# VANA'S ADVENTURE WITH MOTHER EARTH

Dana Petrovic

BALBOA.
PRESS

A DIVISION OF HAY HOUSE

Balboa Press books may be ordered through booksellers or by contacting:

Balboa Press
A Division of Hay House
1663 Liberty Drive
Bloomington, IN 47403
www.balboapress.com
1 (877) 407-4847

Print information available on the last page.

ISBN: 978-1-5043-3334-4 (sc)
ISBN: 978-1-5043-3335-1 (e)

Balboa Press rev. date: 08/14/2015

To N., S., K., S., A. and A.

One of Vana's favourite activities is to visit her grandmother's farm because it has always offered her so many different things to see than she was used to experiencing at her parents' home in the city.

There were also new places to discover and especially many more secret hiding spots available to her. And, as with any city girl being on any farm, it was a never-ending source of delight for Vana to run after the chickens, collect their eggs and softly stroke cows' faces while looking into their friendly, deep-brown eyes.

As a special treat for all of Vana's visits, Granny would get up very early on the first morning to prepare Vana's most-loved breakfast of farm fresh eggs and homemade cured bacon from neighbours. This was served with Granny's own jam and hot bread straight from the oven.

Granny also made this first morning breakfast a special tradition by always putting two items at the very centre of the breakfast table. First, there would always be hand-picked flowers from the garden arranged perfectly in a crystal vase. And second, right next to these flowers, Granny always remembered to place the red leather covered drawing journal to be used for Vana's visit. This journal was always next to a newly-sharpened graphite pencil.

One of Vana's favourite routines whenever she visited was to take her journal with her on her explorations to sketch some of the birds and flowers she saw and to write down some of her thoughts. Vana's many previous journals were so precious to Vana, and also to Granny, that they were always left at the farm for safe-keeping.

There was one more very special morning ceremony at Granny's but this one was celebrated on just about every morning of Vana's visits. Once breakfast was ready to be served, Granny would give the go-ahead signal to her Beagle puppy *Elvin* that it was now okay to scamper into Vana's bedroom and jump-up onto her bed and lick her face until she was wide awake and ready for breakfast. Vana was always very amused by this ritual even though Granny often said, "I'm sure *Elvin* enjoys this even more than you do Vana."

Elvin

Once up and dressed for the day and after having had breakfast, with Granny busy, Vana was free to secretly take-off in search of new adventures on the farm. And, true to Vana's inquisitive nature, with every visit she became more and more courageous in her explorations.

One day, with Granny busy waiting for an apple pie to finish cooking in the oven, Vana grabbed her newest red leather covered sketching journal and pencil and decided to boldly explore a far-off corner of Granny's orchard that she had not been to before. The orchard is where Granny got all her apples, cherries, pears, plums, various berries and other fruit that she used for juice, made into jams and jellies or stored in the pantry as fruit preserves for her home-made pies.

Orchard

It was a sunny, springtime morning and all of the fruit trees were in full blossom as Vana strolled through orchard grove. She thought that the falling flowers looked a lot like a winter snowstorm and that the once green, grassy ground now appeared to be almost totally blanketed with white and pink snow.

Vana thought it would be an artistic challenge for her to sketch in pencil the details of one of these intricate blossoms but before doing so she found one of the largest and oldest trees and decided to lie down to rest a little under the shade of its low-hanging branches.

Lying flat on her back and looking skyward, Vana was both enchanted and mesmerised by the way the light breeze would cause the blossoms to float away from the branches. She giggled whenever one landed directly onto her face. She then deliberately closed her eyes tight so that she could just feel, and hopefully perhaps also smell, any more blossoms that might happen to fall directly upon her forehead, eyelashes or cheeks.

It seemed like only a few moments had passed when Vana felt something tenderly touch her eyebrows when brushing away some of the fallen flowers. She knew this sensation was definitely not from a blossom so she opened her eyes and was surprised to see, gazing down upon her, one of the most beautiful women she had ever seen in her whole life. What also amazed Vana was that she did not feel startled or afraid. In contrast, she only felt very safe perhaps because the woman's warm smile somehow made Vana feel protected.

"Did I fall asleep? And, whom might I ask are you?" Vana asked, only out of curiosity, for she still felt no fear whatsoever.

"I am *Gaia*. And, you must be Vana," the woman expressed in a soft and welcoming voice.

"I was just lying here in my Granny's orchard with my eyes closed feeling these fruit blossoms fall onto my face. Hey, I don't mean to be rude but how did you know my name?"

"Don't be alarmed. Although we have not been formally introduced I have known you for a long time and thus I am so very glad you have visited your grandmother's orchard today. It is always a special pleasure for me to see young girls like you stop and take the time to experience such simple joy as feeling something as soft and pure as fruit blossoms falling upon your face. It saddens me that there are far too few children, and especially adults, who don't take - or make - the time for such pleasures."

*Gaia* paused briefly. "Vana, I have noticed on many occasions that you do have an extraordinary curiosity, an adventurous spirit and a special talent and because of this I would like to invite you to go on a journey with me to visit my castle and some other very special places and friends of mine?"

"You have a castle!" Vana exclaimed feeling a little confused but still no fear.

"Are you some kind of queen?" Upon saying this, Vana started to get very excited for she had always loved stories about queens and princesses.

"No, Vana. I am not a queen as you know it. As I said, my name is *Gaia* but most people simply refer to me as Mother Earth." After seeing Vana's puzzled face she added, "I can better explain who I am if you wish to join me on our little journey."

Vana thought to herself and then said, "A journey? But my Granny will miss me and also be terribly worried if I stay away for too long."

*Gaia* responded, "I promise it won't take very long. In fact, it will seem to be over shortly after it begins. Come with me. We'll start at my castle. And, I promise to return you safely, to this exact same spot, under this very same tree, right here in your Granny's orchard."

Vana, still feeling no fear, followed Mother Earth, now hand-in-hand, deeper into the orchard. Near the far end of Granny's property, they came upon the largest apple tree that Vana could have ever imagined. The tree trunk was so wide at its base that it actually had a wooden door carved into its bark. Mother Earth, with just one finger, touched this door and it mysteriously opened revealing a stairwell descending down, and through, a maze of tangled tree roots into what appeared to be an underground castle.

*Gaia*, still comforting Vana by gently holding her hand, led her down the stairs and sure enough they soon found themselves within the walls of an underground castle. Vana found the massive rock walls fascinating.

Reaching out and placing her tiny hand on one of these enormous rock walls Vana asked, "How could anyone be so strong to move and shape such gigantic rocks to make all these walls?"

"As you will soon experience, Vana, I have many more secrets for you to discover. Let us continue our journey. As you will see, there are many more mysteries I would like to share with you today."

After walking through a large empty room that made their footsteps echo off of the stone floors and rock walls, they came to the end of the room and faced a castle wall that had a doorway entrance into another arched passageway that appeared to lead them even deeper underground.

Just after entering into the deep darkness beyond this archway Vana became startled for the first time since meeting Mother Earth when she thought she had heard a soft whisper addressing her. It sounded as if it was simply saying, "Vana" and this murmuring sound felt as if it had encircled her from all sides of the rock walls. She did her best to ignore the whispers and, holding Mother Earth's hand a little tighter for reassurance, Vana continued on the journey.

Although there were no electric lamps anywhere to be seen, their path was surprisingly brightly lit. It was as if a pure light was coming out of Mother Earth herself who continued to lead Vana by her hand down into the winding web of corridors. She radiated strength and determination.

"Where are we?"

"Vana, we are now quite deep down inside my castle, my kingdom, my home - The Earth."

"I don't understand. I didn't think that anybody could survive underneath the ground because we cannot breathe down here."

"That is only partially true Vana. It is true you humans are not really supposed to live down here. However, some of your animal friends love it here because their bodies are designed to survive here. For example, moles actually call this dark, damp earth their home."

Vana had heard of moles only once before. She remembered her grandmother once complaining about moles piling-up mounds of freshly dug soil on the ground in Granny's orchard. However, Vana had never even seen a photograph, or even a drawing, of one before.

*Gaia* waited patiently for a few moments and then excitedly pointed with her finger, "Look! Why there's a mole right now. I know almost everyone around here by name so let me personally introduce you to *Guaca*. Look closely Vana. I am quite sure he is smiling at you."

Guaca

Now, Vana seeing a mole for the very first time almost shivered at the sight of it and uttered, "But he is so ugly!" Guaca's smile turned into a sad grimace.

"I don't agree Vana. *Guaca* is absolutely beautiful." Mother Earth did her very best not to visibly reveal any disapproval at Vana's negative observations about one of her family and after a momentary hesitation, *Gaia* said, "I want to introduce you to more of my friends. Come with me."

This time they took another corridor and, after a long walk, Mother Earth abruptly stopped. "Do you recognise what these are Vana?"

They were standing in front of what looked to be just a wall of mud and stones but because of the radiating light coming from *Gaia*, Vana was able to see many sparkling colours.

"These are precious gemstones. When I built my underground castle many of these gems got scattered under the surface of the Earth in many distant places around the world. Humans were then able to more easily find these radiant stones. Unfortunately, this has not always worked out so well."

Mother Earth paused and then purposely turned her face away from Vana for she did not want to let the young girl see the deep disappointment in her eyes that she felt about how humans had behaved so greedily after discovering her precious gemstones.

Mother Earth made eye contact with Vana again. "I am truly glad you humans cherish so many of my precious creations. I just wish that many more of you would love my other children as much as you, for example, hunt and dig for my gems." She then stretched out her arm and pulled from the muddy wall a dazzling, bright stone.

"Is that a diamond?" Vana's mouth dropped at the sight of the large, sparkling stone.

"Yes it is. This is one of my gifts that you humans really do genuinely love. Indeed, you almost worship them and, in fact, have actually both killed and died for them. Yes, they are clearly beautiful! I should know for I have created them.

However, I have also created to sparkle just as brightly the morning dew on blades of grass in the dawn's early light. Regretfully, so few of you humans ever seem to notice. This is probably because dew is perishable and, therefore, you feel you cannot selfishly possess it."

Mother Earth continued, "Oh, how you humans love to own things! In my opinion, crystal-like dew drops should be even more precious than diamonds, green emeralds or red rubies. Why? You have to wait for the next sunny morning, just after a morning rain or a heavy dew, to see water drops glitter like this again.

And, when they do sparkle again, they also share with you not just one colour but every colour of the rainbow! I know you are very young Vana. Perhaps too young to understand how I feel? However, I also know that you have a special talent to understand these things which is why I have invited you to come with me today."

"Yes, maybe" Vana shyly admitted. She was a little embarrassed that she didn't really comprehend why Mother Earth was so saddened by something as beautiful as these gems that she alone had created. However, Vana also accepted that *Gaia* was likely correct. She was still very young and, therefore, she did not blame herself for not fully understanding.

"It is okay Vana. One day you will understand all of this because you are smart, very curious and, above all, also a very sensitive girl. Perhaps, I shouldn't have shown you my deep disappointment about my gems so early on our journey. Please forgive me."

Vana didn't really know why she was supposed to forgive Mother Earth. Furthermore, she had never before met any adult, other than her Mom, Dad or Granny, ask her for forgiveness for anything.

Mother Earth exhaled one last sigh and then, beginning to feel a lot better, began looking ahead again to the journey. "Perhaps I should have showed you things in a better order. Since you have now already met *Guaca* and also seen my glittering gems, there are many other children of mine who are just as lovely. Do you still want to meet them?"

Vana enthusiastically nodded her head. "Yes, please, of course."

The next castle corridor provided another pathway of rock stairs except this pathway winded back up towards the Earth's surface. The climb was so quick that Vana actually had problems breathing normally again when she finally reached the fresh air.

The sun was shining brightly in a cloudless, azure sky and, after also regaining her vision again, she realised they were now standing in the middle of a huge grove of many different kinds of fruit trees. It was even more splendid than her grandmother's orchard.

Vana immediately recognised these fruit trees and, unlike those in her Granny's orchard which were still in blossom, these were already filled with ripened fruit. Both she and *Gaia* took a long moment to simply pause and watch the butterflies playing in the breeze and also listen to the insects and birds buzzing and flying back and forth from tree to tree.

Mother Earth then, it seemed to Vana, began looking for just one special type of tree. After inspecting many trees, she finally stopped under one of the tallest trees in the orchard and pulled down on one branch so that she could pick a specific fruit.

*Gaia* hid two of these fruits within her closed palm and then cracked open one of them with just the sheer power of her beautiful hands. She then opened her hand to reveal both the broken shell and the intact fruit for Vana to see. Vana wondered how such slim and delicate fingers could have so much strength and agility.

"Look Vana! What is this inside this broken shell?"

"It's a walnut! I know this. My grandmother also has a walnut tree next to her barn. We pick them directly from the tree, and also off the ground, every autumn and then crack them open to eat the nuts immediately or to save them in the kitchen for baking."

"Yes, you're correct. But it is much more than just a walnut. What else could it be? Look with your imagination - and maybe also with your heart - at the walnut in my palm."

Vana didn't know what to *look with her heart* actually meant but Mother Earth must have somehow secretly inspired her for she suddenly saw much more than just the walnut's hard, brown shell outside and its soft, tan-coloured nut inside. For the first time Vana took the time to thoroughly inspect the fine delicate lines on the shell's surface and the symmetry of its fruit inside.

"It is like art," whispered Vana.

"I knew you would see it this way Vana. Art! A true masterpiece if I don't say so myself."

Now, Vana was starting to see a simple walnut as if she could actually begin to see with her imagination and her heart.

"Since you like it so much, tell me of what it reminds you?"

"Why, it looks almost exactly like the human brain! I've seen drawings of the brain in Science books at school." Mother Earth seemed very pleased with Vana's insight.

"And I have more for you." She reached this time to another tree and picked a bright yellow fruit that she opened again.

"And what about this?"

"That is a lemon." Vana was proud that she knew the answer.

"Yes, it is. And what does it remind you of?"

"Of a flower?"

"Very good!" Mother Earth seemed pleased again. "This is fun! Now, you might not know this fruit because it doesn't grow in your area." This time, Mother Earth moved few steps toward another tree and picked yet another fruit. Its purple colour made Vana think of a plum, but the skin was not as smooth as that of a plum. The skin of the fruit reminded Vana of an eggplant.

"This you humans call mangosteen. You probably haven't seen it before because it originates from Indonesia and needs more sun than the trees you know in your area. Look!"

Again, Mother Earth opened the fruit and disposed its white content.

"What do you think?"

"It looks like a bird nest."

"Exactly! It does. Very good observation.

"And how about this one?" This time, the Mother Earth pulled a fruit that Vana immediately recognised, even before the Mother Earth opened it and exposed its green surface with little black dots.

"This is a kiwi."

"Well done. And of what does it remind you?"

Vana didn't know at first, until she looked into the green eyes of Mother Earth.

"Well, it sort of looks like an eye."

"You are so smart. It does look like an iris. And it is another sample of my artwork. Sometimes, I cannot stop starring at the beauty of my children." Mother Earth lovingly observed the fruit in her hand. "What does this tell us?"

Vana wasn't sure how to answer this question. All she knew was that she wanted the game to continue. "Mother Earth. Can you show me some more samples?"

"There are many, many more examples Vana. After today, just continue to look out for them every single day. Let's continue our journey now."

This time *Gaia* guided Vana so quickly across, and over, the surface of Earth that Vana felt like she was flying, not unlike when she travelled with her parents by plane. And just like from within an airplane peering out the window, Vana could see lakes, rivers, mountains, valleys and maybe even an ocean blur by beneath them. However, Vana was not on a plane and yet here she was flying! She felt strange that she didn't feel she had to use any of her own strength to fly - like a bird would have to do by flapping its wings.

When they descended and eventually stopped with their feet firmly planted back on the ground, they stood in an old town square where an imposing tree was circled by park benches and rusty, iron railings. The tree had an ancient, weathered trunk that seemed to be almost as wide as the town square itself.

Vana knew the tree was ancient because its branches, some as thick as regular tree trunks, had become so heavy that they were threatening to break off. To prop them up, some townspeople had put wooden poles underneath for support.

"Do you know what this is?"

"Hmmm. Well, it's a tree?" shyly offered Vana.

"Yes. But what kind of a tree?" *Gaia* smiled

"A very old tree", Vana added. It was clear that Vana not only didn't know what kind of tree this was but that she also didn't want to admit not knowing. So *Gaia* graciously stepped-in and answered her own question.

"It is a Linden tree. And, you are correct Vana. It is indeed very old and she has seen much in her many, many days spent here on Earth. If she were to speak to you now, she could recite many of the fables you humans like to tell. I mean the sort of stories that you call your history.

I brought you here because this tree is a dear, old friend of mine. And, in the spring, her fragrance is like one of the sweetest perfumes on our planet. And, look, her leaves are shaped like hearts. Her name is *Tilly* and she and I want to share something very special with you."

They waited patiently for a few minutes but nothing happened. Then, almost as if Mother Earth had personally willed it, a strong gust of wind blew directly through *Tilly's* branches and leaves. Suddenly, the sky above the village square, and Vana's head, was filled with whirling little figures resembling little airplane propellers or helicopters.

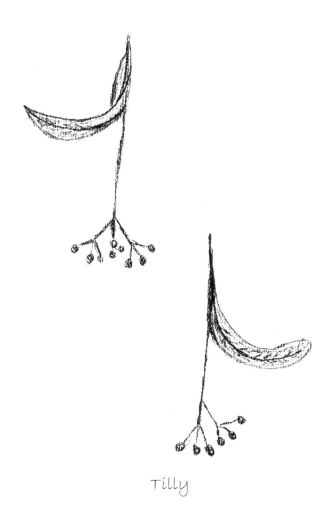

Tilly

Despite not knowing the precise name of this tree, Vana did know that these must be seeds from the tree. Vana was hypnotised by their grace. In addition to looking like propellers, they reminded her of dancing ballerinas gracefully performing pirouettes in the air as they eventually made their way to the ground.

"Have you ever seen such an incredible dancing performance before Vana?"

Vana responded to this question with only a smile. She sat down on the closest nearby bench and continued to follow with her eyes their flight patterns. One of them danced across her face and bounced off her nose before landing directly between her feet on the cobble stones.

Then, a second gust of wind produced an encore performance with even more seeds this time starting to take their maiden flight. Another soon closely passed by her face and this time it tickled her ear and Vana could have sworn that it had actually whispered to her as it flew by, "Hello Vana."

As curious as Vana was about this she also wondered how this could even be possible. After all, it was only a seed and even though Vana knew she did not have many answers for all of Mother Earth's questions today, Vana did know for certain that seeds could not talk!

Mother Earth, who had actually heard the seed say hello to Vana, was closely observing Vana's response. *Gaia* did not seem too surprised that Vana did not mention anything about a seed whispering in her ear. After all, Mother Earth was very patient, especially since she knew that Vana's journey had only just begun.

Vana was not sure how much time had passed but they soon rose again effortlessly into the sky and resumed their adventure. Not too long thereafter they returned to the Earth and found themselves under another stately tree but this time it was not in a town square but in a deep, lush forest.

To Vana's astonishment, this tree's trunk seemed several times wider than *Tilly's* trunk. And, the tree itself was also much, much taller than the Linden tree. In fact, it towered so high above Vana that she couldn't see the top even when she put her head all the way back to look up. For everyone, not only for Vana, the very top of this tree would rarely be seen for it almost always disappeared into the clouds.

"This, Vana, is one of my oldest friends. It is a Sequoia tree. And, yes she also has a name. I simply call her *Big Red*. As you can see, she is definitely *Big*!"

"How is it that *Big Red* has become one of your oldest friends", Vana whispered with both awe and genuine interest.

"Vana, she has been with me here on Earth for a long, long time. *Big Red* won't admit exactly how old she is - she is after all a lady - but I know she is almost 3,000 years old! Do you realise that she has been offering safe homes for animals, birds and insects since before you humans invented the alphabet that you use today to read and write?"

*Gaia* continued, "*Big Red*, thankfully, is very, very lucky to still be here with us today because many of her younger brother and sister Sequoias - and her children - despite also being nourished by me for thousands of years have been killed by humans with axes and chain saws in only a few, short hours! Just like that!"

*Gaia* loudly snapped her fingers to dramatically show the swift speed of the Sequoia's destruction and this sound seemed to echo over and over again within *Big Red's* branches.

Vana continued to stare up at the huge tree trying, in vain, to see the top. She only gave up when her neck started to hurt too much. She had never before seen a tree like the Sequoia *Big Red*. She was looking forward to telling her grandmother about it because Granny loved all kinds of trees so much. Vana, naturally, was also very anxious to tell her grandmother about Mother Earth and all of the adventures Vana had shared with her.

Suddenly, a "Welcome Vana" loudly boomed out from somewhere within *Big Red*. Vana thought she was just imagining things but then this exact same greeting of "Welcome Vana" was soon repeated. Vana looked around but the only other person nearby was Mother Earth who appeared to be quite amused by Vana's puzzled face.

"I am quite sure that *Big Red* is trying to talk with you Vana," *Gaia* deviously said.

Vana looked up to see how this could be possible. She also noticed that the Sequoia seemed to be moving its branches almost as if they were arms waving hello. Vana discreetly waved back and then, feeling very silly because she knew that trees, as with seeds, definitely could not speak, she blushed red in the face and dropped her arm down.

"I have known you for a long time Vana even though we have not been introduced until today." This time Vana definitely knew she had heard *Big Red* talk and all this was becoming a little too much for Vana to understand or accept.

"How could you possibly know me? I have never been here before." Anger began to rise in her. She felt that *Big Red*, and maybe even Mother Earth, might be playing some sort of trick on her and she did not want to appear stupid.

"That is not entirely true, Vana. Even though you have not actually been here, your breath has reached me here many times before.

Whenever this happens, I take in your breath and exhale it, sending back to you the fresh air that your lungs need to keep you alive. I do the same thing for your Granny, Mom, and Dad and of all your friends. So, you see, I have actually known you since you took your very first breath as a new-born baby. Does this make any sense?"

Vana responded by simply saying, "No, I'm sorry but I don't really understand. All I do know is that Granny has always told me that the trees on her farm help make the air fresh and clean. But I have never really thought about what happens to my breath after it leaves my lungs."

Vana, now realising that she was actually involved in a real conversation with a tree, that also had a real name like *Big Red*, glanced upwards again toward the top of the tree to maybe see from where the words were coming. However, the very top of the tree remained lost in the clouds.

My Granny has been right, once again, Vana thought. Trees are important for our fresh air. However, I never knew before how, or why, we are so directly connected to trees.

Feeling a little less confused, Vana now turned to ask Mother Earth a question.

"I never knew that trees could speak." The tone of her voice expressed some doubt because she somehow still feared that *Gaia* might burst out laughing and tell her not to be so silly.

Instead, Mother Earth took her face into her gentle hands and said, "They communicate with you humans all the time but far too many of you have become deaf to their words and no longer listen to their cries. As a result, entire forests have disappeared. And, just like with my gemstones, some humans think they have a right to own, buy and sell what were supposed to be my gifts to everyone here on this Earth."

*Gaia* continued, "Too many no longer seem to appreciate that trees not only create fresh air for humans but that they also provide homes for so many animals and even some plants on this Earth. Yet, humans continue to cut trees down - without any replanting of new trees - to produce wood or paper. Or they do it to simply open up acres of empty fields. All of this upsets the delicate balance of life I have created on this Earth."

"I am so sorry Mother Earth. I did not know so many of these things before I met you today."

"I know my dearest Vana but you don't need to feel sorry for me because I am very strong. You should rather feel sorry for your fellow humans. That is why I have personally chosen you to see what we have seen so far on this journey. You see, I know that your curiosity and sensitivity will help you understand about what has been going on here lately. There is much more to discover. Come with me. Our next stop is very, very close to here."

They had only taken a few steps along a path when Vana looked down and exclaimed, "Mother Earth. Look. What a beautiful flower!"

"Yes, it most certainly is. Again, I am not surprised that you noticed it and that you like it so much. But look a little closer. In addition to us being here, this flower also has another visitor hiding in its colourful, scented petals."

"It is a bee!" Vana was pleased to show that she still knew some things about nature (thanks mostly to her Granny!). Then, as if they had disturbed the bee's work, it quickly left the flower and flew away.

"Did we scare it away?"

"The bee? Why should it be scared?"

"Because maybe we frightened it," Vana offered as an explanation.

"No, it is definitely not scared. It simply has too much to do. I bet it probably did not even notice us, otherwise, I am sure it would have said hello. Oh, by the way Vana, this bee is a *he* and he also has a name. His name is *Bizzy*."

Bizzy

They tried to follow *Bizzy* by sight but he was so fast that it was difficult to keep track of him. Eventually, they saw that *Bizzy* had reached his beehive home in the hollow of a nearby tree.

Mother Earth spoke again, "The reason I wanted you to meet *Bizzy* is because bees, and many other insects such as butterflies and ants, are some of my most important helpers here on Earth. They are not only some of the smallest ones but also often the most hard-working."

Mother Earth paused. "I will explain why. Take *Bizzy* and his friends. These little hard-working bees land inside flowers to eat sweet nectar. Then, the bees' fuzzy legs and bodies get covered in a sticky powder called pollen. When the bees go from flower to flower to eat nectar they leave behind some of the gluey pollen from previous flowers deep within the next flowers. This is called pollination and it necessary for the flowers to grow into the fruit, nuts and vegetables you humans eat. Unfortunately, as with *Big Red's* family and all my forests, far too many bees are being killed by humans."

"How are we doing this? And, are a lot of bees dying *Gaia*?" wondered Vana.

"Well, you humans now live mostly in cities where you do not have many flowers so bees have less nectar to eat. Plus, even in the countryside, your farmers are now using chemicals called insecticides or pesticides which are fancy names for something that is specifically designed to kill insects that may harm harvests. However, these same chemicals also make bees become weak, sick and often die.

If this continues, you humans - and your Granny - will not be able to grow fruit in your orchards and farmers will not be able to produce other food."

Vana replied clearly understanding the results, "This will not only mean no more fruit from my Granny's trees but no more of her fruit pies! What can we do to save these bees from dying?"

"The easiest thing for everyone to do, even you children, is to plant lots of flowers so that the bees, like *Bizzy* here, will have pollen to eat and transfer from flower to flower. This will make it easier for the bees to help flowers grow into the fruits, vegetables and nuts that will keep you naturally healthy."

"My Granny already plants lots of flowers. I have seen bees there before but I did not know how important they were. I will start growing more flowers with my Mom and Dad at our house in the city" offered an enthusiastic and always eager to help Vana.

"That will be a great help Vana. Did you know that bees, in their home beehives, also create a very healthy food that some of my other animal friends, and also you humans, simply love to eat. Do you know what food bees make?"

"Of course! One of my favourite books when I was much, much younger was about a silly bear that could never eat enough of this food that bees make. It is called honey."

Mother Earth paused while observing some activity in the forest just in front of them. "That's right. If you would like to watch a bear trying to get honey from a beehive, all you have to do is look over there right now!"

Vana quickly looked up and, sure enough, there was a young black bear that had just found the hole in the tree where *Bizzy* and his friends had built their beehive. Before Vana could realise what was happening, the bear had swiftly shoved his big paw deep into the hive and had taken it out again. The paw was now totally covered with a dripping, gold-coloured honey.

The bees - and *Bizzy* - naturally got very agitated but the bear had obviously decided that any temporary pain from bee stings was well worth the long-lasting sweet taste of this honey.

Mother Earth called out, "*Ursus*! That is not very polite. You should apologise to *Bizzy* and the other bees."

*Ursus*, with his paw now stuffed all the way into his mouth, mumbled something that sounded like, "I apologise."

Ursus

"No. Not to me. Say you are sorry to the bees!" Mother Earth pointed her index finger toward the angry bees but *Ursus* was so content tasting his honey that he simply turned his back to Vana and *Gaia* and slowly walked away upright on his two back feet so that he could continue to lick his honey-covered front paw.

Mother Earth shrugged. "I must apologise to you again Vana. I should have first introduced you to *Ursus* especially because, as you can see, I am trying to teach him the importance of manners. For example, he and most other bears never ask the bees for permission to eat the honey or, at the very least, warn them. What can I say? Sometimes, even I cannot change some of the bad habits of animals even though I created them."

Gaia signed and paused for a moment while still looking in direction of *Ursus*.

"Vana, did you know that insects not only help flowers grow into fruit but that they are also food for many of the birds I have created. So, you see, I not only love insects because they work so hard but by also being food for birds we can enjoy hearing birds sing their songs. Haven't you heard them singing today?"

Prompted by *Gaia's* comment, Vana finally noticed birds singing from everywhere all around them. It sounded like a chorus and Vana concluded that they were all singing so loudly because they wanted to impress *Gaia*.

"Birds don't only sing Vana! They do other important work for me as well. Some of them, like hummingbirds, also transport sweet pollen from flower to flower. And, many other birds help carry seeds from trees to far, far away open spaces where these seeds can grow into new trees. As you saw earlier with *Tilly* the Linden tree, some trees use the wind to send their seeds far away. But many trees need the help of birds."

"How do birds spread the tree seeds?"

"Oh, there are many ways. When trees drop their seeds or fruit onto the ground birds can see or even feel the vibration. The birds then eat the fruit which may also include the seeds. The birds then - how shall I say this politely - drop the seeds onto open ground.

"Or, they drop directly onto my dad's car but only after he has just washed it!" laughed Vana.

Mother Earth chuckled at Vana's joke and then continued, "And, I have even created some trees that have seeds with a strong scent that attracts insects. And where there are insects, there are birds ready for a feast. You see, to make the balance of life work easily on my Earth, I try to make things as simple as possible for my family."

"Wow! That is incredible!"

Just then, a little chickadee landed on a tree branch close to Vana and Mother Earth.

"Hello Vana, nice to see you again."

At first Vana, naturally, was once again surprised but after having already experienced speaking seeds, trees and bears now listening to a small bird talk no longer seemed so shocking!

"Hello to you, also. Do you have a name?" asked Vana trying to impress Mother Earth with her polite manners and continuing so positively with the conversation.

"Yes, my name is *Sunny*. I am told by my parents that they gave me this name because even as a baby bird I loved eating sunflower seeds all day long and now, more importantly, I always try to have a cheerful or *sunny* personality."

Sunny

Vana continued with the conversation. "And, when and where have we seen each other before *Sunny*?"

"Well you fed me and my whole family last winter at your Granny's farm. It was a very cold and snowy winter. Do you remember? You put bread and seeds out in the bird feeder each time you came to visit. We tried to thank you with our songs but you didn't seem to listen. Maybe it was because it was so cold you quickly ran back into the house to keep warm."

Vana glanced at Mother Earth, feeling very proud that she had helped feed *Sunny's* family. *Gaia* simply smiled back as if to say, "You see! Your work was not in vain."

Vana didn't really know what else to say. After all, she didn't have much experience having conversations with birds. Thankfully, *Sunny* seemed content to simply thank Vana once again for the food the previous winter by filling the silence with loud, non-stop chirping and singing.

They continued to listen to *Sunny* as they resumed their journey by walking deeper into a forest. Soon *Sunny's* song became so faint that they could barely hear it. The type of trees around them began to change. Everything was very damp and wet because of a now constant rain. The trees were so thick at their tops that their leaves blocked the daytime sun and it became very dark. Fallen, rotting branches and thick vines were blocking Vana's every step but *Gaia* continued to help Vana and together they managed to pass over the branches without ever slipping or falling.

"I hate the rain", Vana blurted out. A colourful macaw flew over their heads as if Vana's words had scarred it. Vana thought for a moment that she had heard the parrot call out, "Don't say that. Don't say that. Don't say that."

This didn't surprise Vana as much as seeds, trees, bears and other birds talking because Vana knew from TV that parrots could actually mimic the talking sounds of humans."

"And, why don't you *like* rain?" Mother Earth's asked deliberately not repeating the word *hate*.

"Because I cannot play outside with *Elvin* and hunt for new adventures when it rains," Vana quickly answered.

"Ah yes *Elvin*. He is such a cute puppy. But do you not see how alive and diverse this forest is Vana?"

Vana only nodded because she considered the question rather silly for there was nothing else around them but forest.

"You may not realise this but this kind of forest is actually called a *rain* forest and it therefore needs a lot of water for its growth. It is home to many, many hundreds of different animals and other species I have created. If it were not for the heavy rain these creations would have no other place to live for they depend entirely on a constant, rain supply. Yes, you might not be able to play with *Elvin* when it rains outside at your Granny's farm but these animals and plants wouldn't survive without a lot of rain. Now, hopefully, you may want to reconsider your choice of the word *hate* when referring to rain?"

Vana didn't respond to *Gaia's* question because she felt a little ashamed. She felt foolish for having said she hated rain and she wished she had thought her answer through more wisely before responding so quickly.

Mother Earth remained silent for a moment allowing Vana to have the time to reflect and then she grasped Vana by the hand, quickly but also calmly and they then took off from deep within the dark dampness of the rain forest to fly up into the open sky.

They continued to rise high up until *Gaia* and Vana eventually stopped to rest within one of the clouds that had been, only a few moments before, dropping buckets of rain on their heads when they were on the ground in the rain forest. However, despite the cold temperature, Vana's face felt refreshed and she realised for the first time that she actually enjoyed the sensation of the rain drops caressing and cooling her skin.

"Nice to see you again Vana", a very deep voice from somewhere close by within the cloud thundered. By now, Vana was no longer even the least bit surprised when any of *Gaia's* friends spoke to her.

"Again? So, have we met before?" Vana courteously enquired of the rain cloud.

"First, I should introduce myself. My closest friends call me *Lono*. I know it is a somewhat unusual name but it comes from the Hawaiian name for the god of rain."

"I like the name *Lono*. And, as with my name, it is very easy to remember. *Lono*, can you please tell me when we met? I don't remember", Vana asked again with genuine interest.

"Of course. We have met many times but the last time was only a few weeks ago when you were visiting your grandmother and you were at the rain water pond just behind your Granny's house. I remember that you were watching your own face reflecting back to you, like from a mirror, on the surface of the pond.

You were there to fill your watering can to help your Granny water her garden. I was very proud of you for helping. I then came directly over your Granny's farm, darkened the skies and added a little thunder and lightning - only to politely announce my arrival of course. I guess I chased you back into the house. I hope I didn't scare you too much."

Vana felt proud now that *Lono* had noticed that she had helped Granny. She felt even prouder knowing that her willingness to help her grandmother had always happened without ever being asked. Vana was also becoming more and more proud about her grandmother because of her wisdom about, and her love for, Mother Earth.

Vana's regret at using the word *hate* was still visible in her face and slumped shoulders. *Gaia,* wanting to brighten Vana's spirits, helped her climb further up from within *Lono* to sit comfortably on his fluffy surface where they were now exposed to a blue, warm and dry sunlit sky.

"You are a wonderfully sensitive girl Vana so I am sure you felt that it surprised me to hear you chose a word like *hate* for the rain." Vana was about to protest that this was not what she had really meant - at least not anymore - but Mother Earth continued.

"All living creatures on Earth need water to live and they wouldn't have anything to drink - or eat - if it were not for *Lono* giving us his gift of rain. Try to imagine no lakes, rivers and oceans in which to swim. Or worse, no water to drink or no water in the rain pool behind Granny's house. No rain would mean no flowers and, therefore, none of your grandmother's favourite fruit pies. Now, what would life be like without Granny's pies?" enquired *Gaia* with a returning cheeriness in her voice.

Instead of answering, Vana continued to remain respectively silent.

"I do not mean to cause you any worry Vana - or to lecture you while on this journey - but very recently, here on Earth, humans have contributed to some very harmful developments. And, sadly far too many of my children who I created long, long ago have already forever disappeared from our Earth."

"What are we humans doing to cause this?" asked Vana innocently.

"Well, that is a complicated topic that has generated a lot of arguments. However, I do know that much of the recent harm has been, in a large part, caused by humans burning the oil that is buried under the ground and ocean floors. You are burning this oil so that you can run your cars, engines and factories and also heat, and cool, your houses.

However, burning so much of this oil has also caused heat and gases to float upwards into the atmosphere, far above where we are now comfortably sitting on *Lono* and burn away the protective shields that were created to protect you from the hot, burning rays of the sun.

In response, Vana simply sighed and eager to hear more, despite the gloomy prospect, let *Gaia* continue.

"However, rather that expressing to you in more words let us look at a very dry and hot - but still also breathtakingly beautiful place - where the hot sun almost always shines and where there are very few clouds to make rain. By visiting such a place, we should get a better idea how life might tragically become in more and more places here on Earth.

For this part of our journey, I will ask another dear friend of mine to help us get there. And this time, unlike with *Ursus* the bear, I won't forget to introduce you. My friend's name is *Khamsin* but I simply just call him *Hamsin*. You know him by what he does. *Hamsin* is the *wind*."

"*Hamsin*? Are you anywhere nearby? We need your help."

And, almost as if *Hamsin* had been idly waiting just nearby for *Gaia's* next command, he started immediately to blow and thereby gently push Vana and Mother Earth who remained sitting atop of *Lono*.

"Oh. Hello *Hamsin*. I believe you, like many of my friends we have seen today, have met Vana before?"

*Hamsin* answered with a cooling and breezy voice, "Yes, I have even played with her several times. Hey Vana! Do you remember losing your hat in my wind on the way to school a few weeks ago? Well, that was me! And, I've done this quite a few times to you before because I know you love to wear hats. I have enjoyed playing these games with you."

Vana remembered this recent school incident and also several other episodes in the park with her parents, or at her Granny's farm, when she had lost her hat in the wind. Now, she knew why.

"You know Vana" Mother Earth continued, "*Hamsin* is another one of my great helpers. I don't know what I would do without him."

*Hamsin* replied very modestly after hearing these compliments. "I am always here to help you *Gaia*."

"Thank you *Hamsin*. Now, can you, with *Lono's* assistance, kindly help us get back down so that Vana can get a closer look at the amazing art work you have created?"

When Mother Earth and Vana landed, they did not land on a hard rocky ground or on a grassy field but on the soft sands of an endless desert. The landscape, in all directions as far as the eye could see, was shaped by sand dunes and this time it was a very hot and dry air that was making it very difficult for Vana to breathe, not to mention that the hot sand was burning her feet.

"*Hamsin* is a true artist who has formed all these splendid sand dunes but he is never, ever happy with his result. This is why he goes on, and on, and on, continually reshaping them. They are so beautiful, aren't they? Vana, part of the reason there is so much sand here is that it hardly ever rains. Do you think you would be able to live here?"

Vana, still having a difficult time breathing in the hot, dry air, could only shake her head sideways indicating a definite "NO!"

"You may find this difficult to believe Vana but I have many of my children living quite happily in this extremely hot and dry environment. They've found a way to survive. Some have learned to stay out of the hot sun and protect themselves in the shade during the day. It is daytime now so you won't see any bats, snakes, rodents or larger animals like foxes and skunks because they always sleep in the day in cool caves, dens or burrows and go out only at night when it is much cooler."

Vana was not saddened by the fact that she will not see any rodents, bats and snakes.

"You humans may not be able to survive here long without water but I have helped many animals survive here by giving them special abilities in the same way that I helped *Guaca* the mole with special capabilities to be able to breathe underground.

For example, some of my children have learned to actually get moisture from the fog that I sometimes send to them. And, one of my favourite desert friends is the Kangaroo Rat which lives underground in dens which they seal closed at both ends. They then recycle from their own breathing the moisture necessary to survive."

It was so hot and dry that if these tales of animals being able to actually live in this desert had been told to her by anyone other than Mother Earth herself, Vana would not have believed these stories.

Meanwhile, *Hamsin* had long ago stopped listening to Mother Earth and he had already begun reshaping some more dunes on the horizon that seemed to interest him much more than *Gaia's* stories. Mother Earth couldn't help but notice.

"*Hamsin*, thank you so much for helping us to get here. We are now going to visit another great master who, like you, never feels that an artist's work is ever finished."

*Hamsin* remained busy reshaping the dunes and Mother Earth didn't seem to really mind that he was no longer paying any attention to her.

Vana was totally surprised when *Gaia* now said, "Let's continue our journey by enjoying the desert for a little while longer. Let's begin walking together in that direction across one of *Hamsin's* sand dunes."

"But Mother Earth! I still can't breathe very well because it is too hot for me here. My feet are also burning on the hot sand and I'm already really, really thirsty." Vana pleaded.

"Vana, you can trust me. I am sure we will find a solution to this lack of water and extreme heat problem very soon."

Not more than a minute later, after reaching the summit of one of *Hamsin's* smaller dunes, Mother Earth pointed out something appearing just at the bottom of the dune. "Look there Vana. It's our next stop on our journey."

Vana could hardly believe her eyes for she could now see just below her a beautiful valley and in its middle a flowing river with tall, green trees following its banks. She rubbed her eyes over and over again to refocus her eyes and to make sure it was not a mirage.

They walked only a few more moments and then sat down next to each other on the sandy beach shore of the river where they both soon became mesmerised by the fast moving, sparkling-in-the-sun surface.

In addition, the entrancing sound of the flowing water soothed Vana and made her immediately forget that she had been so hot and thirsty only a few moments ago. She was hypnotised by the small currents and circling eddies that were formed wherever the river met rock obstacles hindering its path. Vana felt she could watch these pools of water and listen to their sound for eternity.

The solitude and silence was eventually broken by *Gaia*.

"Just like *Hamsin*, a river never seems to be content with the results of her art. Her flowing force moulds the landscape like an artist transforms clay into a sculptured statue. Mountain ranges are penetrated and deep valleys are formed. I admire rivers so much and, therefore, I am honoured to have rivers as some of my very best friends starting with this river before us right now!"

"Vana, I would like to introduce you to *Nadi*."

*Nadi*, having been formally introduced, politely replied in a gurgling voice, "It's my pleasure to meet you Vana. As proud as I am of this valley I have formed around and through these mountains, *Gaia* has asked me to show you today how much life there is beneath my surface. You may not realise this but there is as much - if not more - life thriving here within my waters than on the surface of the Earth. Would you like to meet some of my friends that live below my surface and deep within my waters?"

Before Vana was able to say anything, they were already under water and she was again, hand in hand, following *Gaia's* lead. She obviously couldn't breathe through her nose or mouth but she surprisingly didn't feel the need to do so. It was actually very relaxing. And, even without any goggles, she could see very clearly with her eyes wide open. It must have been just another one of the many tricks - like flying - Mother Earth had already performed on their journey.

Sensing Vana's trust and resulting calm, *Gaia* said, "Promise me to never try to do this when swimming alone or with your friends or parents. I have not created you humans to breathe under water.

Today, and only with me at your side, will you have this ability but after returning to Granny's, or with your parents or friends, it will be dangerous if you try to breathe under water again. Please promise me, Vana?"

Vana did not hesitate to nod affirmatively. Without the magical powers of Mother Earth protecting her, she knew that she would die very quickly if she stayed under water too long.

And, as Vana had learned to expect from so many of *Gaia's* friends on this journey, one of the river residents began to talk with her.

"Hello Vana. My name is *Pearl*. It's very nice to finally meet the girl who loves the scent of lemons so much."

Even though Vana was still underwater she could not only see very clearly but she could also listen very easily. Thus, she was able to look in the direction of the voice to see that this time it was a dark-coloured, thick-shelled river mussel that was talking to her.

Pearl

"It's my pleasure to meet you *Pearl* but how in the world did you know I love the smell of lemons?"

"Well that's easy for me to explain but maybe not so easy for others, except for you, to understand. You see, river mussels like me are very, very sensitive to the water conditions in the rivers wherein we live. This is, tragically, why many of the man-made chemicals humans have dumped into lakes, rivers and oceans have already killed so many of my family.

But, let me answer your question more directly. You use soaps, shampoos and water to wash and bathe. And, you also use detergents to wash your clothes and dishes  Have you ever wondered what happens to these soapy waters after they drain from your sink, bathtub or washing machines? Well, they often go into sewers and then directly into rivers like *Nadi* where I and my whole family feel these cleaners pass over and even through us in rivers.

For example, I know your mom, dad and you like to use body soaps and laundry detergents that smell like lemons. I know this because these artificial fragrancies make me feel *dizzy* and often very sick."

"My soaps? You have felt the soaps I use." Vana had never thought of what happened to her soap or indeed any of her used water after it left her bathtub because her primary concern had always been for her to be as clean as possible. Vana was now beginning to realise that she ought to also help others to protect their health.

"Yes, everything you consume or use that leaves your home through water pipes eventually drains right into our home. So, Vana, think of me - your new friend *Pearl* and my family - the next time you drain or flush water and its contents away from your home."

"I will. I will", Vana promised with the second "I will" intending to show *Pearl* she really meant it.

Listening to this discussion and waiting for a break in the conversation, *Gaia* politely interrupted, "You have to admit Vana that rivers are one of my greatest creations. In addition to meeting *Pearl,* and what you probably already know about rivers, there is one thing you may not have noticed about all rivers."

She paused for a moment to be certain of getting Vana's full attention, "They all flow in the same direction - down towards the sea. Isn't that brilliant? So, shall we now let *Nadi* take us to the sea? It's not far. All we have to do is just relax and go with the flow! I will continue to make sure you can breathe. Just continue to hold my hand and let *Nadi's* currents guide us to the ocean."

Vana simply smiled showing her agreement and then they both just let go and drifted just beneath the surface of the river until, not much later, they found themselves at the coast.

Vana knew they had arrived at the seaside because the fresh water was now mixing with the shoreline's salty waters. And above *Nadi's* surface, as she remembered from her family vacations, she could now see many sea gulls hovering just above the water looking to quickly plummet and catch any fish that might have come too close to the surface.

Vana then found herself in the middle of a complex system of tree roots. Still underwater, she looked up above the surface and noticed that these roots belonged to a type of tree or bush she had never seen before.

"What kind of tree or plant is this Mother Earth? It has green leaves and branches like other trees or bushes but it also has naked roots that are entirely in the water and not soil," Vana uttered.

Mother Earth grinned widely at Vana's use of the word *naked* to describe these roots.

"These trees, I must admit proudly, are one of my most clever creations. They are called mangroves. I placed them along coasts all around the world. They are unique because they can survive in both the fresh water from the rivers and the salty waters of the ocean.

They are also known as the protectors of the shoreline because they stop tides and storms from washing away the land. Their complex system of roots are also great places to hide so they also help protect many animals such as shrimp, crabs, fish and even the close cousins of *Pearl* - sea mussels.

"It's too bad they don't survive on land", Vana offered.

"Why would you want them on the land?" replied *Gaia* curiously.

"Because I also love to find places to hide. Hide and seek is my favourite game," answered Vana with a slight giggle she could not suppress.

Mother Earth looked fondly at her mangroves appreciating what special things they do to protect the coastline and so many of her creations.

"And I am truly very happy when my children are protected because I love all of them, including you, my princess." She smiled directly at Vana who immediately felt like she had grown a few centimetres taller due to such an open expression of love from such a strong and marvelous woman.

Still remaining under the water, they then continued to let the river's current take them farther from the coast and out deeper into the sea.

Soon, Vana was absolutely delighted to be able to actually swim under the water right alongside many schools of fish. Their colours were so vibrant and shimmering that Vana could not help but think how wonderful it would be to be a fish.

"They are all so beautiful."

"Yes, I have worked very hard - and for a very long time - to create so many species of fish but it has been well worth the effort. They are truly lovely. But wait! What is happening just over there Vana?"

Over by a huge underwater formation that looked like a human brain - similar to the walnut *Gaia* had shown her previously - Vana saw an enormous fish arguing with a similar-looking but quite smaller one.

Then, *Gaia* motioned to Vana to swim closer to get a better view of the quarrel. When they finally did get closer, Vana realised, to her pleasant surprise, that she had not actually seen two fish.

"Mother Earth, it's a killer whale and a dolphin! My two favourite sea *mammals* because, just like us, they breathe air and have warm blood!"

"Vana, I knew you loved dolphins and orca whales so I sent them a special invitation to meet you here today. However, I didn't expect they would be so rude to fight with each other about who would be best to show you around their underwater neighbourhood!" explained a somewhat disappointed *Gaia*.

"Stop fighting you two! Is this how you present yourself for the first time to our special guest?"

They stopped the argument and greeted their guest more politely with both saying at the same time, "Welcome Vana!"

Then only the dolphin spoke. "It is my honour to introduce you to my friend *Yakki*. *Gaia* told us you know a lot about dolphins and killer whales so you probably already know he is an orca whale. We call him *Yakki* because he never stops talking, or singing, or yakking."

Yakki and Clicker

"Thank you for such a friendly introduction. Please allow me to return the favour now", responded *Yakki.*

"This is my dolphin cousin and my closest friend. He also likes to talk a lot by using clicking sounds which is why he has earned the nickname *Clicker.*"

"Hello *Yakki* and *Clicker,*" Vana said cheerfully."I have met many of Mother Earth's friends today who have said they had already known me. Do you two already know me as well?" she asked boldly.

*Yakki* answered first. "No, not really. Neither of us have had the pleasure to meet you before. But *Gaia* told us that you loved orcas and dolphins and, naturally, we immediately volunteered to show you around."

"Yes that's true," added *Clicker*, "but Mother Earth also told us that we would meet a special visitor who likes adventures. This is why I was really looking forward to meet you. I also love adventures because I think that all of life is nothing but a long, single adventure. Do you also see it that way Vana?"

Vana was a bit stumped for an answer. *Clicker* then realised why.

"Hmmmm, I should have noticed that you are still very young Vana. However, one day when you get as old as me - I am 48 years old - you will better understand what I mean. Until then, just try to enjoy each and every day as a new adventure because no new day will be the same as any of the days that have already passed by."

"I certainly will *Clicker*", replied Vana confidently for she already knew she enjoyed adventures a lot - maybe even too much - as her Granny would often say.

"Well *Yakki* and *Clicker*, thanks for your warm welcome and advice but have you found the perfect, lovely sea forest that I asked you to find to show Vana today?" intervened *Gaia*.

Instead of answering, both Yakki and Clicker enthusiastically nodded their heads up and down, swam quickly to the ocean's surface, rose into the air, excitedly hit the water with their tails, took a deep breath of fresh air and then finally came underwater again to swim endless circles around *Gaia* and Vana showing that they both wanted to personally escort Vana to the sea forest.

They then swam effortlessly through the water with both of them using their strong tails with Vana and *Gaia* trying to keep up. Vana couldn't take her eyes off of their graceful yet powerful bodies.

Soon they all arrived at what looked like to be an underwater forest but, unlike the one on the land earlier where Vana had met *Big Red*, this forest appeared to be in its autumn glory with all the leaves golden yellow and red.

"I am very proud of this forest. After creating so many of the colourful fish that you swam with earlier, I knew I also had to create many more shelters where these fish could safely hide when they were in deeper water far away from the mangroves.

This forest is actually called a coral reef and it provides shelter for little fish and other small creatures that can easily hide in there."

Vana looked closely into the wavering branches and leaves of the coral reef and sure enough she soon saw countless small fish hiding undetected in the shadows.

Mother Earth proudly continued, "Even though coral reefs cover only a small portion of my ocean floor, many of my sea children live in these reefs. They also provide a protective barrier between the oceans' storms and the exposed shorelines."

Vana listened intently to *Gaia's* valuable information and it occurred to her that Mother Earth told these stories with the same pride that all mothers or fathers would have telling stories about their own children.

With Vana still busy peering into the sea forest, *Clicker* snuck up behind and pressed his nose against Vana's cheek. Vana giggled uncontrollably which pleased *Clicker* so much that he once again raced upward to the water's surface and did a double somersault, back flip in the air.

"I am quite positive that *Clicker* just gave you a kiss. He seems to like you a lot. And, I am equally sure that *Yakki* would have done the same if he were not so big."

"That's true. I don't want to scare you Vana. Even though I did not kiss you it does not mean that I have not enjoyed meeting you today," said *Yakki* sincerely.

"It's time we should be going" both *Clicker* and *Yakki* said again at the exact same time. This made everyone laugh bubbles and then, with the wave of both their dorsal fins and tails, Vana's two new, special friends said goodbye and disappeared into the darker depths of the ocean.

Mother Earth, having just introduced to Vana her two favourite mammals, now knew it was time that they should soon end their journey.

"We should get you back to your grandmother soon, don't you think Vana?" recommended *Gaia*.

And even though Vana would have loved to continue with this incredible adventure, she could not disagree.

"Yes, Mother Earth. You are probably right, again. I don't know how long but I am sure we have been gone a long, long time. Granny is probably getting very worried by now."

As Vana had learned to expect and appreciate, *Gaia* again took her by the hand and together they made their way back to the shore where they finally left the water and walked up onto a pebbly beach. Vana had been under the water for so long that she felt she had to learn to breathe fresh air all over again.

They followed a sandy path from the beach that led them uphill into an orchard of old apple trees. *Gaia* purposefully started heading toward one particular tree.

Once Vana saw the tree, she immediately realised that it looked identical to the huge apple tree with the wide tree trunk that Vana has entered with *Gaia* earlier when their journey had started. And, this tree also had a similar wooden door that Mother Earth simply pushed open again with just one finger. And soon, just like earlier, Mother Earth was directing Vana down a stone stairway and into a familiar labyrinth of stone walls and tree roots.

"Well, well. Look who is still here!" Mother Earth exclaimed trying to sound genuinely surprised.

Vana looked up and saw none other than *Guaca* the mole busily eating something.

This time, Vana remembering that she had said that *Guaca* was ugly, attempted to make up for her early mistake by greeting *Guaca* with a special, warm hello.

"Hello *Guaca*. Nice to see you again. Have you had a nice day?" said Vana.

"Hello to you also Vana. A nice day you say? Has it really been so long ago since we met?" replied a somewhat puzzled *Guaca*.

Mother Earth was very pleased to hear Vana be so courteous to *Guaca* but soon continued to lead Vana onward for the journey was quickly coming to a close.

It was not long before Vana recognised the enormous rock walls that provided the very foundation to *Gaia's* underground castle.

Then Vana unmistakably heard again whispers from the rock walls saying, "*Hello Vana.*" This time she decided not to ignore them (after all she had grown accustomed to listening to moles, seeds, bees, birds, bears and even clouds and rivers talk with her).

"Mother Earth, who is it that is now whispering to me?"

Mother Earth slowly advanced a few more steps before deliberately stopping just in front of a massive stone wall and cupped her ear with her hand as if listening to the rock wall.

"Well, it is my dear friend *Petra* who is attempting to communicate with you, my dear Vana. I am glad that you heard her this time because, unfortunately, usually stone walls are only appreciated when they maybe have some valuable minerals or metals.

Yet, they are one of the most valuable and oldest friends that I have. Take a look the next time you walk through the nature. Wouldn't you agree *Petra*?"

"Well, Mother Earth, I would humbly agree that I am the foundation for many to live and thrive on Earth and within our seas.

And, I'm glad to see you again Vana especially after your incredible journey with *Gaia*."

Vana smiled and replied, "I am also very glad to meet you *Petra*. I regret not responding to your hello earlier."

Now it was Vana's turn to come close to the solid stone wall and when gently placing the flat of her hand on the wall, Vana was surprised it felt so warm and not cold.

"You are beautiful." Vana uttered and she meant it from the bottom of her heart. Because of her journey she was able to now discover, for the first time, the varied but subtle shades of colour on *Petra's* surface.

"Thank you Vana", replied *Petra* whose voice was now charged with emotions.

Mother Earth was also visibly moved.

"Thank you so, so much Vana. Nobody I have ever taken on a journey like this has ever said, or understood, that my simple - and seemingly dead to most - stone walls are actually *alive* and beautiful.

But I won't get into the depth of this now for I already know you will one day fully understand this Vana and because I promised to return you to your Granny."

After a brief pause Mother Earth continued.

"So, Vana, what do you think about our little adventure today where we met so many of my dearest friends?"

"They were all very friendly. I liked them all. I wish there was more time to meet more of them."

"I knew you would like them. That is why I wanted you to meet them. As promised, we will soon return to the exact same place where we started our journey today because I want you to understand what I sometime call the *circle of life*. We all also need to understand that everything on Earth should be in perfect equilibrium. It took me a long time to create this balance but it has been worth the effort."

"How do you do it?" Vana earnestly wanted to know.

"Do what?"

"Manage all of this. Take care of all of your creations."

"Well, my friends the sun and the moon, help a lot. We make a great team. And, as you saw, I have many other friends such as *Hamsin*, *Nadi* and *Lono* who, as you experienced, are very helpful as well. But to be truthful, if humans helped me just a bit more it would make my job much easier."

"What can we do?"

"Well, you humans are my greatest accomplishment but too frequently also my greatest disappointment. I wish you could be more humble and less selfish in your relationship with me and all of my other children who share with you their lives upon *our* planet."

*Gaia* paused for a moment. It was clear she was choosing her words very carefully.

"Sadly, too many of you no longer see the grace and beauty of my creations. You seldom stop, even for a second, to admire the deep redness of a tomato, the dark green of a spinach leaf, the elegant swaying of a palm tree in the breeze, the splendid scent of an orchid or the inherent beauty within a stone wall. There are so many wonders I could go on forever."

Mother Earth paused again for a second still deliberately searching for just the right words.

"I do love it that humans consume my vegetables, fruit, wheat and even meat from my fish and animals. That is why, in part, I have created all of them in the first place. I only wish you would show more respect by not destroying so many species so quickly. You must learn to understand that if you kill off one family other families will die as well because they depend on each other's existence.

As I mentioned, everything is in equilibrium and there is enough of everything for everyone. I have tried to be very generous to all my children."

Mother Earth let out a slight sigh and it was now her turn to put the palm of her hand on the same stone wall that Vana had just placed her hand.

"I mentioned earlier that I don't want to lecture. I prefer to inspire. This is especially true for you Vana and it is why I selected you to join me on this journey today. I looked for somebody who will understand that you don't need to worry about me because I am strong. I have created a world in which life that supports life thrives and life that destroys life disappears.

My deepest wish is that you discover - every day of your life - just one more of my wonders and then share this miracle with your friends and family. Do you feel that you would like to try to do this by sharing with others using some of your special talents?"

Vana was not certain what special talents Mother Earth was referring to and she could not ask for she was now chocked-up with emotion and barely able to hold back her tears. She knew the journey was about to end and she dreaded the thought of not ever seeing Mother Earth again.

"Don't start to cry my sweet princess. I will always be closely connected with you. When you think of me just imagine that you have roots reaching very deep into me. It is just like *Tilly* and *Big Red*. Only the trees with the deepest roots can survive the fiercest storms.

And, be equally confident that every one of the friends you have met today - *Guaca, Tilly, Big Red, Bizzy, Ursus, Sunny, Lono, Hamsin, Nadi, Pearl, Yakki* and *Clicker* and *Petra* - will also remain close to you.

As you will probably discover - if you haven't already - each of them was carefully selected to teach a very specific and invaluable lesson for your life that you can, one day, hopefully share."

*Gaia* continued, "For example, always be well-grounded with your roots anchoring you just like *Tilly* and *Big Red*. Yet, at the same time, flow with the ever changing currents of life as *Nadi* has done for eternity.

And, when you absolutely believe in something, be as firm and as immovable as *Petra* and her stone walls in my castle. Will you do your best to accomplish this in your life my princess?"

Vana, now damming back a flood of tears, nodded affirmatively again.

And then just as promised, *Gaia* led Vana up the castle stairway, through the door in the apple tree and then back to the exact same spot, under the very same tree in Granny's orchard where they had first met. Mother Earth bent down and embraced Vana with her welcoming arms. Strength and determination filled every cell of Vana's body and she wished Mother Earth would never again let her go. As if feeling her thoughts, Mother Earth tenderly released the embrace and took Vana's hands into hers. Vana felt a small object between hers and Mother Earth's hand.

"Now, my little princess, lie down and close your eyes again just like I found you here earlier. It's time for a farewell but it will not be a final goodbye for my presence is with, and in, you. Be kind to yourself because when you love yourself you also love all that has been created for we are all one entity." This phrase caused *Gaia* to stop and reflect before resuming.

"Yes. We are all one. And, to express my thanks for you joining me today on our journey, please keep this symbol of me as a token of my gratitude. As you can see on the coin-like pendant, I am represented by a circle with a cross and four dots. These dots represent four seasons - Spring, Summer, Autumn and Winter - and also the four elements of life - Air, Fire, Water and Earth. This will help you remember your new friends and me. You can keep it safe in your pocket or wear it attached to a necklace or a bracelet."

Vana clutched tightly the symbol in her right hand and with Mother Earth's farewell words seemingly still resonating in her ears she felt a very familiar and wet sensation on her face.

It was *Elvin* licking her face as he so often did each and every morning. Vana abruptly opened her eyes to not only see the beagle puppy but also Granny looking down on her.

"Hi Vana. I just finished taking the apple pie from the oven and I thought you probably would like a piece. I called for you but there was no answer. So, I got *Elvin* here to help. He, like you, is becoming a very good explorer. He found you pretty quickly lying right here asleep under this tree."

"I wasn't asleep Granny. I only closed my eyes to feel the flower blossoms fall onto my face. But Granny, you would not believe what then happened to me. I met Mother Earth and we then went on a journey to meet some of her children under the ground, in forests, deserts, rivers and oceans. I even got introduced to a dolphin and orca whale named *Clicker* and *Yakki*."

Granny didn't want to dampen Vana's excitement so she responded by saying, "Well, that is definitely a lot to happen in such a short time after I spotted you sneaking off on one of your adventures in the direction of this orchard not that long ago. I knew you hadn't likely gone very far but I still took *Elvin* with me because I knew his nose would find you very fast."

Granny, deliberately changing the topic, simply offered, "The pie is still very hot. This one is made with last year's preserves but by the look of all these blossoms it won't be long before we will have some fresh apples right from this very orchard." Would you like some vanilla ice cream with your pie? I know *Elvin* would?"

Vana knew her grandmother very well and she could tell that Granny didn't really believe her story about her adventure with Mother Earth. However, this was okay. All that mattered was that Vana herself knew she had been on an adventure of a lifetime and that she had just been introduced to *Gaia's* - and now some of Vana's own - closest friends.

More importantly, another reason she didn't really worry about Granny not believing in the adventure was that she had learned today that when she absolutely believes in something, she must be as firm and as immovable in her beliefs as *Petra's* gigantic stone walls within Mother Earth's underground castle.

Finally, she wasn't worried too much right now about whether Granny listened to her story or not because she knew she had many days, months and years ahead of her where she could share with Granny, Mom, Dad and her friends the miracles, wonders and the lessons of life she had personally learned from Mother Earth on this incredible adventure.

So, with Granny now reaching down to offer a helping hand, Vana offered her grandmother her left hand for she was still concealing Mother Earth's gift in her right palm.

Before leaving her spot under the tree, she looked down once more and noticed her new, red-leather journal next to her sketching pencil. Both were now almost completely covered in petals.

She reached down and retrieved both of them. By so doing, she suddenly realised what special talent she had that Mother Earth had mentioned so many times during their adventure. And, it also finally confirmed in her mind and her heart why *Gaia* had invited her on such a special adventure.

So she simply answered her Granny. "Warm apple pie must always be served with vanilla ice cream. It's a Granny's kitchen rule. I would love a piece - maybe even two! Would you agree *Elvin*?"

And, after walking with Granny and Elvin back to the house, Vana, still feeling Mother Earth's constant presence and love, sat at the kitchen table and sketched on page one of her new journal the symbol of Mother Earth from the pendant and just below the sketch she penciled in these first four words:

We are all one!

# ACKNOWLEDGEMENTS

The list of people to whom I am indebted is very long and it doesn't only apply to their contributions to this book but, more significantly rather, extends to their positive influence on my life.

My niece Katarina was the first to give valuable feedback on this book and I am very grateful for her suggestions - and especially her encouragement.

Tanja, my dear lifelong friend who has always supported me, gave me the strength to believe in my work, and thus, myself.

The final hurdle - the dreaded proofreading - was undertaken by Gerry, the love of my life, who stepped-in and corrected all my English grammar and also allowed the ever-present child within him to improve the story.

I am thankful to my father who showed me that being grounded is not merely a trendy status declaration but the only sustainable way of living our lives.

There are of course other family members and friends who gave me encouragement, support and love. I thank all of you. Of note, I must mention my role as godmother to Lynn for, as the words came to me, I often imagined her reading this book one day.

With regard to my drawings, my gratitude also goes to my painting teachers Birgit and Ingrid for their patience and trust in my very humble abilities. Additionally, without my spiritual mentor and rescuer Anja Rahel this wouldn't have been possible. I own a lot of my well-being to her.

Furthermore, I want to thank the kids from my former neighborhood in the Rheingau, Germany with whom I shared such delight and awe when we discovered miracles in my garden. These cherished moments are what inspired me to write this book. I dedicate this book to you.

To all of the above, I am endlessly grateful to - and for - you for I am certain that the world is a better place because you are in it.

Lastly, and certainly not least, I am beholden to Mother Earth for the miracles she allows us to witness every single day.

Made in the USA
Monee, IL
23 April 2021